GIFTED
&
TALENTED®

*To develop
your child's gifts
and talents*

MW01109460

STORY STARTERS

Mysteries

By Q. L. Pearce

Illustrated by K. Michael Crawford

LOWELL HOUSE JUVENILE

LOS ANGELES

NTC/Contemporary Publishing Group

To Chelsea
—Q. L. P.

Published by Lowell House
A division of NTC/Contemporary Publishing Group, Inc.
4255 West Touhy Avenue, Lincolnwood (Chicago), Illinois 60646-1975 U.S.A.
Copyright © 1999 by NTC/Contemporary Publishing Group, Inc.

Managing Director and Publisher: Jack Artenstein
Director of Publishing Services: Rena Copperman
Editorial Director: Brenda Pope-Ostrow
Editor: Joanna Siebert
Designer: Treesha Runnells

Lowell House books can be purchased at special discounts
when ordered in bulk for premiums and special sales.
Contact Customer Service at the address above,
or call 1-800-323-4900.

Printed and bound in the United States of America

ISBN: 0-7373-0204-6

RCP 10 9 8 7 6 5 4 3 2 1

GIFTED & TALENTED® STORY STARTERS: **Mysteries** will help develop your child's natural talents and gifts by providing story-telling and writing activities to enhance critical and creative thinking skills. These skills of logic and reasoning teach children **how** to think. They are precisely the skills emphasized by teachers of gifted and talented children.

Thinking skills are the skills needed to be able to learn anything at any time. Unlike events, words, and teaching methods, thinking skills never change. If a child has a grasp of how to think, school success and even success in life will become more assured. In addition, the child will become self-confident as he or she approaches new tasks with the ability to think them through and discover solutions.

GIFTED & TALENTED® STORY STARTERS: **Mysteries** presents these skills in a unique way, combining the basic subject areas of reading and language arts with thinking skills. Here are some of the skills you will find:

- Deduction—the ability to reach a logical conclusion by interpreting clues

- Understanding Relationships—the ability to recognize how objects, shapes, and words are similar or dissimilar; to classify or categorize

- Sequencing—the ability to organize events, numbers; to recognize patterns

- Inference—the ability to reach logical conclusions from given or assumed evidence

- Creative Thinking—the ability to generate unique ideas; to compare and contrast the same elements in different situations; to present imaginative solutions to problems

GIFTED & TALENTED® STORY STARTERS: **Mysteries** uses a variety of different exercises to help your child develop his or her creative writing and creative thinking skills.

The Fill-in-the Blank Exercises at the beginning of this book will help your child to gain confidence in the story-telling (and story-writing) process. The child has two choices: **a)** to select words from the appropriate Word Lists to drop into the blank spaces; **b)** to use other words or phrases of his or her own choosing to fill in the blanks.

Using the Word Lists expands the young child's concept of what makes a "good" story. It is recommended that the Word Lists be used first, and that you read the stories with your child again, after all the blanks have been filled in. Once the child feels comfortable with the creative freedom to tell his or her own stories, the Fill-in-the Blank Exercises can be reused, with your child providing new words for the blanks.

To help your child grasp the "purpose" and "place" of certain words (like adjectives and nouns), read words to the child from the lists, then ask the child to make up his or her own words instead, words "like" the ones on the lists. Going over the exercises reinforces not only the function of language but its richness as well.

It is important not to be judgmental about your child's choices. The Word Lists reflect the variety of language, so that the child does not form too narrow or too rigid a concept of what is "properly" a hero or "properly" a descriptive word. A child who rejects a Word List and chooses to describe a morning as "yellow" and the hero as a "doorknob" has a very interesting story in the works.

Next you will find Eye-Opening Descriptive Exercises, which encourage your child to pay more attention to his or her environment. Through the use of questions, the activities teach the child to mine his or her own experiences and observations for story ideas. Each exercise stresses the collection of facts for immediate use in an original story. Note-taking should be encouraged. Visual as well as verbal clues and cues are used. If the child makes a visual observation, call attention to it, and/or write it down for later use in the story.

These exercises focus on all five senses to help the child develop his or her ability to write descriptions. Please note that these are observation and description exercises, not writing exercises. It's okay to write down your child's responses allowing him or her to concentrate only on observation. When the child answers a question, ask more questions to draw out even more detail.

After your child completes the Fill-in-the-Blank exercises, he or she will develop an "ear, eye, nose, taste, and touch" for telling a story. The child will be ready for Write the Beginning, Write the Middle, and Write the Ending Exercises. Here, stories are started for the child, who must then provide either the middle or the end. To help your child through the middle of a story, remember that part of a story is a link that provides a logical chain of events from the beginning (provided) to the end (provided). So ask the child to read the ending out loud and imagine what could have happened to lead to such an ending. To help your child through the ending exercises, ask him or her to imagine more than one way the story can end. The more children use their imaginations, the more they will move away from cliches and into creative endings.

The final section contains Advanced Exercises. These provide little help in the creation and writing of each story. The child is given ideas for stories through the artwork or a word box. Please encourage your child to consider his or her initial effort as a first draft. Once he or she has completed an Advanced Exercise and some time has passed, ask the child to expand on the first attempt on another piece of paper. You will both be surprised at how effortlessly the second (and third) drafts become more complete, and even more interesting, stories.

Participate with and read to your children. Help him or her with harder words. A child's imagination should not be limited only to those words he or she can read, since children understand the meaning of words even if they cannot read them. The same is true for those words they cannot write. If necessary, record your child's stories for him or her. Regardless of whether your child can write full, complete sentences, your child will gain much from this book.

Talk to your child about how to write an interesting mystery. Discuss words and phrases that can make a story intriguing. Try to come up with different ideas for creating suspense. Encourage your child to think creatively. Exercising the imagination is what **GIFTED & TALENTED® STORY STARTERS: Mysteries** is all about.

Good luck, have fun, and remember: good writers read, so go to the library often with your child.

Look closely at the entire picture below. Read the story on the next page. Then use the clues in the picture and the story to answer the questions.

CASSANDRA'S HOUSE

Cassandra Little loved the quiet street she lived on. Her house was painted a bright, sunny yellow, which was her favorite color. Her best friend, Samantha, lived in the one-story house next door. Sometimes, Cassandra's cat, Peter, would climb into her room through the window. Even on hot days, her room stayed shady and cool because it was hidden behind the leaves of the big tree in her front yard. She often liked to sit near the window and read. But when she saw other kids from her neighborhood playing ball in the street, Cassandra would race downstairs to join them.

The End

Which house is Cassandra's? _____

What clues in the story and the picture tell you this? _____

_____

_____

_____

What parts of the story are not important for figuring out which house is Cassandra's? _____

_____

_____

How else would you describe Cassandra's house? _____

_____

_____

Many writers use comparisons to make their writing more interesting. A **comparison** shows how two things are alike or different. The words you choose to describe something can make it seem mysterious, scary, or even silly.

Read the example below, then finish the rest of the sentences. Use your imagination to make fun comparisons of your own.

The cat was as black as _____*night*_____.

The house was as gloomy as _____.

The night was as quiet as _____.

The wind howled like _____.

The stranger was as still as _____.

The fog was as thick as _____.

Now choose something that you would like to describe. Write a comparison to describe the object you've chosen. Then draw a picture of it in the box.

_____

_____

_____

_____

_____

drawn by _____

Write a sentence for each picture to help tell a story. Be sure to describe and solve the mystery. When you are finished, read your story out loud.

_____

_____

_____

_____

_____

_____

_____

_____

_____

_____

_____

_____

_____

_____

_____

Complete the story by filling in the blanks. Match the numbers under the blank lines to the Word Lists. Choose words to tell the story and solve the mystery. You can even choose words of your own! Read the story out loud when you are finished.

WHERE'S PROMISE?

By _____

Paula's best pal was her cat, Promise. When the weather

was _____, they played inside. Paula would read to
      1

Promise while he _____ in his favorite flowered
         2

basket. They played outside when the weather was warm.

One _____ spring day, Paula could not find Promise.
     3

She _____ inside the house. He was nowhere to be
    4

found! Paula went outside. Promise's _____ ball was
         5

lying in the _____ grass. But where was Promise?
     6

Paula listened carefully. She heard _____. It was
       7

coming from under the _____ flowers. "There you
      8

are!" she _____, picking up her _____ friend. "I
    9   10

should have known that's where you would be."

The End

Word Lists

(1) cold, windy, rainy, gloomy, stormy

(2) rested, played, curled up, relaxed, snoozed, napped, listened, slept

(3) comfortable, lovely, bright, sunny, nice, cheerful

(4) looked, searched, hunted

(5) favorite, red, colorful, rubber, yarn, small

(6) green, soft, fresh, tall

(7) purring, crying, meowing, rustling

(8) golden, yellow, beautiful, cheery, bright, sweet-smelling

(9) cried, declared, exclaimed, laughed, said

(10) sleepy, dozing, purring, happy, furry

Complete the story by filling in the blanks. Match the numbers under the blank lines to the Word Lists. Choose words to tell the story and solve the mystery. You can even choose words of your own! Read the story out loud when you are finished.

THE MYSTERY OF ELM STREET SCHOOL

By _____

Not much usually happens at Elm Street School. There are

_____ teachers, and there's a really cool _____.
      1   2

But today was _____. I arrived at school in _____.
                        3   4

Some teachers were wearing _____. Others had
                                                      5

_____ in their hair. In class, lots of kids were
                6

talking about _____. I knew that something
                        7

_____ was happening. I saw my _____, Tom,
          8   9

and asked what was going on. "Aliens!" he _____.
                                                                              10

"They've taken over the whole school." "No way!" I

exclaimed. I couldn't believe it! Then I realized it was all a(n)

_____.
        11

The End

Word Lists

(1) nice, excellent, friendly, helpful, far out, offbeat, great

(2) principal, lunchroom, library, playground, swimming pool, basketball court

(3) unlike any other day, strange, eerie, weird, scary, different, fantastic

(4) time, a hurry, the school bus, my mom's car, a weird mood

(5) their clothes backward, funny hats, polka dots, helmets, sunglasses

(6) glitter, flowers, streamers, plastic bugs, grass, shoelaces

(7) spaceships, homework, giant insects, the teachers

(8) bizarre, unusual, curious, odd, mysterious, strange, crazy

(9) cousin, best friend, classmate, pal, friend

(10) whispered, yelled, warned, announced, declared, cried

(11) dream, joke, prank, daydream, gag

Are you ready to try one on your own? Good! Read the story below. It is missing some important parts! Use your imagination and fill in the blanks with your own words. When you are finished, read your story out loud.

THE SURPRISE

By _____

"Look what just arrived!" Louisa's mother said. "It's for you." She showed her a(n) _____ package. "It is from your cousin Thomas in _____." "I wonder what it is," Louisa said. Her mother put the package down on the _____. "Let me see!" her little brother cried. Louisa looked at the package. It was _____ and _____. It was decorated with _____. She carefully picked it up. It was as _____ as a(n) _____! Louisa shook it gently and heard _____. Slowly, she unwrapped the _____. Underneath, there was a plain brown box. She looked all over, but there was nothing _____ on it. Finally, she opened the top. She was surprised to see _____. "_____!" she exclaimed. "It's _____."

The End

Draw a picture that shows Louisa opening her package.
Include her mother and her little brother in the picture.

draun by

Look closely at the entire picture. Then answer the questions on the next page.

How many people are at this picnic? _____

Are there any animals at the picnic? If so, what kind? _____
_____

Is it before or after lunch? How do you know? _____
_____

What is the weather like? _____

What holiday is being celebrated? _____

What activities do the people at this picnic enjoy? _____

_____

_____

_____

_____

Now finish this short story. Make it as mysterious as you can.

THE CASE OF THE MISSING BEACH BALL

By _____

We were having a great day at the beach. In the afternoon, we decided to play a game of catch. I went back to the blanket to get my beach ball. To my surprise, it was missing! Where could it have gone? I wondered. But then

_____

_____

_____

_____

The End

Look closely at the entire picture. Then answer the questions on the next page.

What things can the children in the picture see? _____

_____

What sounds can they hear? _____

_____

What can they smell? _____

_____

What can they taste? _____

_____

What could they touch? _____

_____

Now finish this short story. Make it as mysterious as you can.

A DAY OF FUN

By _____

It had been a fun day at the carnival. We were on our way to the merry-go-round for one last ride. Suddenly, I noticed

_____

_____

_____

_____

_____

The End

Look closely at the entire picture. Then answer the questions on the next page.

What does the picture show? _____

Who is the man yelling from the sidelines? _____

What is the crowd excited about? _____

Where are the Dragons from? _____

Why is the little boy crying? _____

How do you think the game will end? _____

_____

Now write a short story about the picture. Describe what is happening. What is the mystery? When you are finished, give your story a title. Then read your story out loud.

_____
(title)

By _____

_____

_____

_____

_____

_____

_____

The End

Read the story below. It is missing some important parts! Fill in the blanks, then complete the story. When you are finished, read your story out loud. Draw a picture to go with your story in the space on the next page.

THE PACKAGE

By _____

One _____ day, Paul was playing in his front yard. His _____ ball rolled in front of his neighbor's house. "Oh, little boy," he heard someone call. He turned to look. It was his neighbor, _____. She was sort of _____. Paul noticed that she was standing next to a(n) _____ package.

"Would you mind helping me for a moment, dear?" she asked _____. He looked around, then walked up to her porch. The package was _____.

"Careful," she said. "I've been waiting for this package for a very long time." Paul helped her _____. "What is it?" he asked. She looked at him for a minute. Then she asked, "Can I trust you?" Paul took a deep breath. He answered,

_____

_____

_____

_____

_____

_____

_____

_____

_____

_____

The End

drawn by ✎ _____

Read the story below. It is missing some important parts! Fill in the blanks, then complete the story. When you are finished, read your story out loud. Draw a picture to go with your story in the space on the next page.

_____
(title)

By _____

Jeremy got on the _____ bus. The bus began to _____ just as he sat down. He had picked a seat near _____. The bus drove past the _____ and _____.

Suddenly, Jeremy saw something _____. He jumped up and raced to the back of the bus. He could not believe his eyes! "_____!" he shouted. "Stop the bus!" The bus pulled to the side of the street. Jeremy ran straight to the _____

_____

_____

_____

_____

_____

_____

_____

_____

_____

_____

_____

_____

_____

The End

drawn by _____

Read the story below. It is missing some important parts! Fill in the blanks, then complete the story. When you are finished, read your story out loud.

THE COOKIE CAPER

By _____

Jenna was helping her mother make chocolate chip cookies. Her mother _____ took a tray of cookies out of the oven and set them on the _____ to cool. Jenna mixed another _____ of dough. "Let's see how many cookies we have so far," Jenna said. But when they turned to count, the cookies were _____. "Look!" Jenna cried. There was a trail of _____ on the floor. "The cookie bandit must have gone this way," _____ Jenna. Her dog raced ahead. Jenna and her mother followed the trail into the living room and saw _____.

They also found Jenna's older sister, Marie, her little
brother, Peter, and her dog, _____. "Who took
the cookies?" Jenna asked. Then Jenna noticed _____

_____

_____

_____

_____

_____

_____

_____

_____

_____

_____

_____

_____

_____

_____

_____

_____

The End

Read the story below. It is missing some important parts! Fill in the blanks, then complete the story. When you are finished, read your story out loud.

THE CAMP-OUT

By _____

It started on the _____ day of our camp-out. At first, _____ were missing. Tyler noticed that his _____ was gone, then Mark said his _____ had disappeared. That night, we _____ around the campfire and _____. We sang songs and _____. Before we went into our tents, we left _____ near the _____. The next morning, we started to fix

_____ and _____ for breakfast. _____ had disappeared! "What is happening?" Tyler asked Mr. Wheeler. "Who is taking things from our camp?" Mr. Wheeler thought for a moment. "Who or what?" he said. "If we want to _____, we have to _____. Here's what we will do: _____

_____

_____

_____

_____

_____

_____

_____

_____

_____

_____

_____

_____

_____

_____

_____

_____

_____

The End

Look closely at the entire picture below. Then use your imagination to answer the questions on the next page.

Use your answers to these questions to complete the story on the next page.

What time is it? _____

Where is this house? _____

Who is the woman in the downstairs window? _____

What is she doing? _____

Who is the girl in the upstairs window? _____

How old is she? _____

What did she do before she went upstairs? _____

What is she writing about? _____

What is the relationship between the woman and the girl? _____

Who is the man walking up to the house? _____

What is he there for? _____

What is in the briefcase? _____

Read the story below. It is missing some important parts! Fill in the blanks, then complete the story. Read your story out loud.

THE VISITOR

By _____

It was _____ at night. _____ had just finished _____. Slowly, she _____ up the stairs. She was thinking about _____. She sat down at the desk and pulled out a pen. As she was _____, she heard footsteps on the path that led to the house. She knew that _____ would answer the door. She heard a man's voice, but she could not _____ what he was saying. Quiet as a(n) _____, she crept to the top of the stairs. She _____ down at the door. She could see

_____

_____

_____

_____

_____

The End

The beginning of this story has already been written. Write the middle and the ending to complete the story. Read it out loud when you are finished.

THE TREASURE MAP

By _____

Rachel found the paper crumpled between two books in her father's bookcase. At first, Rachel didn't know what it was. It was clearly very old. When she looked at it more closely, she recognized some of the buildings in her neighborhood. It was a map! *I think I know where that is!* she thought. But what did the **X** mean? Was treasure hidden there? She knew she should put the map back, but she couldn't bring herself to put it down. _____

_____

_____

_____

_____

_____

_____

_____

_____

_____

_____

_____

_____

_____

_____

_____

_____

_____

_____

The End

Draw the map that the girl in "The Treasure Map" found.
What buildings should be included? Where does the **X** go?

drawn by _____

Read the story below and look at the pictures on the next page. Finish the story, then draw a picture on the next page. Color the pictures when you are done.

THE ROOM AT THE END OF THE HALL

By _____

"This is boring," Taylor whined. "I hate museums!" He dropped into a nearby chair. "You can't sit there," Rosa said, pointing to a sign. "It's part of the museum's exhibit. The sign says that Thomas Jefferson once sat in that chair." Taylor sighed. "He couldn't have been as tired as I am! Let's try to find the rest of the class." He stood up and started walking toward a door at the end of the hall. "That's off limits," a voice warned. Taylor turned around to face a big man wearing a guard's uniform. "OK," Taylor responded. "We were leaving anyway." The guard disappeared down a different hallway. Taylor turned back to the door. "Let's see what's inside!" he said. "You can't do that!" Rosa cried, but it was too late. Taylor twisted the knob and the door slowly creaked open. _____

_____

_____

_____

_____

_____

_____

The End

drawn by

Look closely at the entire picture. Then answer the questions on the next page.

Use your answers to these questions to help you write a story on the next page.

Who is the girl in the picture? _____

_____

What is her name? _____

What has she found? _____

Where is the boy going? _____

What is the man doing? _____

What businesses are on the street? _____

_____

What sounds does the girl hear? _____

_____

What are the people on the street talking about? _____

_____

Who lost the item that the little girl found? _____

_____

What will the girl do next? _____

_____

_____

_____

Now write a story about the picture. Use your answers to the questions to help you. Describe what is happening in the picture and who the people are. Be sure to write about the mystery. When you are finished, give your story a title. Then read your story out loud.

_____

(title)

By _____

_____

_____

_____

_____

_____

_____

_____

_____

_____

_____

_____

The End

This story has a beginning and an ending. Read the words that are given, then write a middle for the story. Read the whole story out loud when you are finished.

THE LETTER

By _____

Tommy had finished all his chores for the day, except one. He hurried out to the mailbox to bring in the mail. He couldn't wait to go for a ride on his horse, Ginger. _____

_____

_____

_____

_____

_____

_____

He looked at the date on the envelope. It had been mailed 20 years ago! But how could that be? Who was it from? he wondered. He turned the envelope over in his hands, then slowly tore it open. He was nervous as he pulled the paper from the envelope. He could not wait to read it!

The End

Think about the story you've just written. Use your imagination to answer the questions below. The answers will help you with the exercise on the next page.

Who is the letter from? _____

How old do you imagine the person is now who wrote the letter? _____

What does the person who sent the letter look like? _____
_____
_____

Where was the letter sent from? _____

Who is it supposed to be for? _____

What is the letter about? _____
_____
_____

Why did it arrive so late, and where has the letter been since it was first mailed? _____
_____
_____

How does the boy feel when he receives the letter? _____
_____
_____

Now write the letter that the boy found.

_____
(date)

Dear _____,

_____
_____
_____
_____
_____
_____
_____
_____
_____
_____
_____
_____
_____
_____
_____
_____
_____
_____
_____

Sincerely,

_____

This story has a beginning and an ending. Read the words that are given, then write a middle for the story. Read the whole story out loud when you are finished.

THE MYSTERY ACT

By _____

"Attention," a voice called over the speaker. "May I have your attention, please. The show will be starting in just a few minutes. We apologize for the delay." Margie turned to look at her cousin Kenny. "I don't think I can wait much longer! What do you think is going on back there?" They looked up at the stage. Suddenly, there was a loud crash.

_____

_____

_____

_____

_____

_____

_____

_____

_____

_____

_____

_____

_____

_____

_____

_____

_____

_____

_____

_____

_____

_____

_____

_____

_____

_____

_____

_____

_____

_____

_____

"Well, I guess we solved that mystery!" Margie laughed. "That wasn't so hard!"

The End

This story has a beginning and an ending. Read the words that are given, then write a middle for the story. Read the whole story out loud when you are finished.

WORLDS OF WONDER

By _____

It was strange to see two moons hanging in the night sky. Lots of things were odd about Pax Seven, Todd thought. Still, he was glad to be there. This was the first time that his dad had ever brought him along on a business trip to another planet. He planned to make the most of it. While his dad was in a meeting, Todd walked around the hotel. Suddenly, he heard a noise on the path behind him. He spun around and came face-to-face with _____

_____

_____

_____

_____

_____

_____

_____

_____

_____

_____

_____

_____

_____

_____

_____

_____

_____

_____

_____

"I will never make that mistake again!" Todd exclaimed. Although he had to go home to Earth, he knew that he would someday return to Pax Seven.

The End

This story has a beginning. Read the words that are given, then write a middle and an ending for the story. Read the whole story out loud when you are finished.

THE MYSTERY OF THE OLD LIGHTHOUSE

By _____

Tanya was very happy that her parents had rented a house by the beach for the summer. From her bedroom window, Tanya could see the ocean. She could also see an old lighthouse in the distance. The neighbors said that it hadn't been used in more than 50 years. It was locked up tight and would soon be torn down.

　　One evening, Tanya was looking out her window. Suddenly, she saw a bright light shining from the top of the old lighthouse. "I thought it was deserted," she whispered to herself. _____

_____

_____

The End

This story has a beginning. Read the words that are given, then write a middle and an ending for the story. Read the whole story out loud when you are finished.

THE ABANDONED HOUSE

By _____

Charlie and Carrie were best friends. They lived just down the street from each other. Every day, they raced each other to the end of the block. The winner got to decide what they would do for the rest of the afternoon. One day, as they were about to start their race, Charlie said, "Let's explore the old house at the end of the block." Carrie did not think that was a good idea. They had raced past the house hundreds of times, but they had never dared to go inside.

Suddenly, Charlie yelled, "Last one there is a slowpoke." He started running. Carrie ran after him as fast as she could. Charlie didn't usually beat her, but today he had a head start. They stopped outside the broken fence and watched the house for a minute. "Let's go inside," Charlie said. "Look!" Carrie cried. _____

_____

_____

_____

_____

_____

_____

_____

_____

_____

_____

_____

_____

_____

_____

_____

_____

The End

This story has a beginning. Read the words that are given, then write a middle and an ending for the story. Read the whole story out loud when you are finished.

THE DIARY

By _____

Andy stayed with her grandmother for a month every summer. Her grandmother lived in a big old house in the country. It had a large shaded porch where Andy and her grandmother would sit and talk.

One afternoon, while they were sitting outside, her grandmother fell asleep. Andy sat quietly for awhile, but then she grew restless. She went inside the house to find something to do. She walked down the long hallways, stopping to look out the windows. Suddenly, she reached the door to the attic. She had never been inside before. Without thinking, she reached for the doorknob. The door creaked open, and _____

_____

_____

_____

_____

_____

_____
_____
_____
_____
_____
_____
_____
_____
_____
_____
_____
_____

The End

This story is missing a beginning and an ending. The middle of the story is already written. Read the words that are given, then write the beginning and the ending. When you are finished, give your story a title. Then read your story out loud.

_____
(title)

By _____

_____

_____

_____

_____

_____

"It's starting to rain!" Timmy yelled to his friend Josh. "Quick! In here," he said. He pushed open the door and they rushed inside. The wind pulled the door shut with a bang. It was dark inside. Timmy could not see very well. "Hello?" he called into the darkness. _____

_____

_____

_____

_____

_____

_____

_____

_____

_____

_____

_____

_____

_____

_____

_____

_____

_____

_____

_____

The End

Look closely at the entire picture. Then write a story to go with it on the next page. Don't just describe the picture. Write about the mystery. Who is in the tree house? Why? What will the boy and girl do? When you are finished, give your story a title. Then read your story out loud.

_____
(title)

By _____

_____
_____
_____
_____
_____
_____
_____
_____
_____
_____
_____
_____
_____
_____
_____
_____
_____
_____
_____
_____
_____
_____

The End

Look closely at the entire picture. Then write a story to go with it on the next page. Don't just describe the picture. Write about the mystery. Who or what does the girl see in the mirror? What will she do next? When you are finished, give your story a title. Then read your story out loud.

_____

(title)

By _____

_____

_____

_____

_____

_____

_____

_____

_____

_____

_____

_____

_____

_____

_____

_____

_____

_____

_____

_____

_____

_____

The End

Read the words listed below. Write a story using ALL of these words. They can play a big part in your story or just get a quick mention. But all of the words must be found somewhere in the story. Have fun! When you are finished, give your story a title.

DOOR   WHISPER   GLOVES   ENVELOPE   MISSING

_____
(title)

By _____

_____

_____

_____

_____

_____

_____

_____

_____

_____

_____

_____

_____

_____

The End

Read the words listed below. Write a story using ALL of these words. They can play a big part in your story or just get a quick mention. But all of the words must be found somewhere in the story. Have fun! When you are finished, give your story a title.

STORM   **CANDLE**   **CURTAIN**   **CAT**   **WINDOW**

_____

(title)

By _____

_____

_____

_____

_____

_____

_____

_____

_____

_____

_____

_____

_____

The End

Everyone has different ideas about what makes a good mystery. What do you think? Write a short story about a place that you think is mysterious. Then draw a picture of it in the space below.

A PLACE OF MYSTERY

By _____

_____

_____

_____

_____

_____

_____

_____

_____

The End

drawn by _____